Juliana H. G. Ewing, Elizabeth S. Tucker

Leaves from Juliana Horatia Ewing's Canada Home

Juliana H. G. Ewing, Elizabeth S. Tucker

Leaves from Juliana Horatia Ewing's Canada Home

ISBN/EAN: 9783337188900

Printed in Europe, USA, Canada, Australia, Japan

Cover: Foto ©Andreas Hilbeck / pixelio.de

More available books at **www.hansebooks.com**

LEAVES

FROM

JULIANA HORATIA EWING'S
"CANADA HOME."

Some homes are where flowers forever blow,
  The sun shining hotly the whole year round;
But our home glistens with six months of snow,
  Where frost without wind brightens every sound.
And home is home, wherever it is,
When we 're all together, and nothing amiss.

                                    J. H. E.

LET COME WHAT WILL COME
God's will be wel come

Yours v. truly
Juliana Horatia Ewing.

LEAVES

FROM

JULIANA HORATIA EWING'S

"CANADA HOME."

Gathered and Illustrated

BY

ELIZABETH S. TUCKER.

TOGETHER WITH FACSIMILES OF EIGHT WATER-COLOR DRAWINGS
BY MRS. EWING'S OWN HAND.

BOSTON:
ROBERTS BROTHERS.
1896.

TO

Margaret Medley,

CONTENTS.

LIST OF ILLUSTRATIONS.

Leaves from
Mrs. Ewing's "Canada Home."

CHAPTER I.

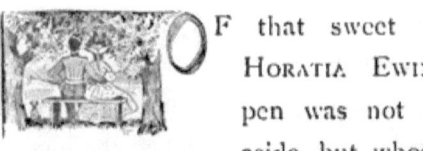

F that sweet writer, JULIANA HORATIA EWING, whose busy pen was not long since laid aside, but whose memory lives with us in the pages of some of the best loved and brightest stories in the English language, these are a few memories and facts of that portion of her life spent on this side of the Atlantic, — a sort of gleaner's sheaf, from the rich field of that life already gone over and stored by her sister, Miss H. K. Gatty,[1] who, however, in her interesting work has left almost untouched the record of the two years in Canada. So that with the aid

[1] "Juliana H. Ewing and her Books," by Miss H. K. Gatty, 1885.

of loving memories held by her many old friends
there, together with some of her own charming
letters written " Home " at that time, we have
many things of interest to tell.

In the small provincial city of Fredericton, New
Brunswick, she spent two years of her earnest
life, writing there many of her sweetest stories;
and we find, in following her footsteps and in
reading her letters, how deeply she loved the quaint
old town whither she came, a stranger and a bride,
with her husband, Major Ewing, when his regiment, the twenty-second of England, was ordered
there in 1867.

Her dearest friend there, Margaret Medley, wife
of the late Bishop Medley of Fredericton, has
been to me a veritable " Mrs. Over-the-Way "
in giving me of her " remembrances," as little Ida
in that story would say; and to her thanks are
due for the delightful letters, as well as the
interesting set of water colors drawn by Mrs.
Ewing's own hand.   These were done, in fact,
especially for her revered and beloved friend the
Bishop of Fredericton, and were given to him

on her departure for England.   Her love and
esteem for these two friends can readily be seen
by the frequent mention of them in these letters
" Home."   It was to them she dedicated her book,
" A great Emergency," and she keenly enjoyed
her study of Hebrew with the Bishop, who in his
turn was greatly impressed by the quick mind
and retentive memory of his pupil.

Mrs. Ewing is described as having an earnest
face, with deep set, "thinking eyes," while her
slight form seemed almost too frail and small to
carry the abundant crown of golden hair worn in
plaits coiled at the back of her head.

Can one not almost see her, sitting as in her
photograph here, that earnest face bending over
the papers on her lap, — writing, writing, writing
the lovely thoughts which flowed so readily and
continually from her magic pen?

The Ewings occupied three or four different
homes during their two years' stay in Fredericton,
but the favorite one was that which I can see from
my window here, with its three gray old willow
sentinels.   She often speaks of this house in her

letters, how much she enjoyed her life there. She called it " Reka Dom " — House by the River, — for it stands on the bank of the river St. John, across the road from three old willows. There she wrote her story of " Reka Dom," and here is a sketch of the window in her room, — probably the very one by which she sat when writing.

Once when she and her husband were walking on the river bank not long after their arrival in Fredericton, seeing this old shambling house — which she describes in one of her letters, — she expressed a wish to live in it; and they moved there as soon as they could get possession. How she must have enjoyed the beautiful St. John River flowing in front of their windows, guarded by the rows of old willows! Her room is in the lower right-hand corner, with the closed shutters.

I think that dog " Nox," in " Benjy in Beastland," must have had his " improvised morgue," for the " bodies " he found in the river, under that very old willow which still stretches out over the river its " finger-like " leaves. This is what she says

MRS. EWING'S HOUSE, "REKA DOM."

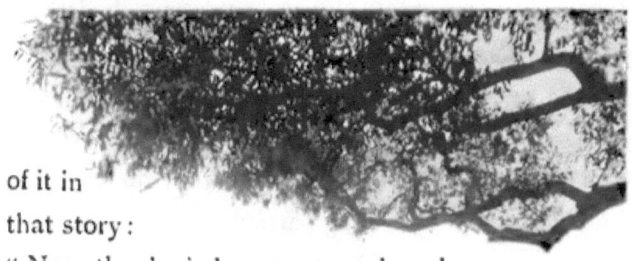

of it in
that story:

" Near the dog's home ran a broad,
deep river. Here one could bathe and swim most
delightfully. Here also many an unfortunate animal found a watery grave. There was one place
from which (the water being deep and the bank
convenient at this spot) the poor wretches were
generally thrown. . . . Hither at early morning
Nox would come, in conformity with his own
peculiar code of duty, which may be summed up
in these words: 'Whatever does not properly or
naturally belong to the water, should be fetched
out.' . . . Not far from the spot I have men-
tioned, an old willow tree spread its branches
widely over the bank, and here and there stretched
a long arm, and touched the river with its
pointed fingers. Under the shadow of this tree
was the morgue, and here Nox brought the

2

bodies he rescued from the river, and laid them down."

This river was a great source of joy and pleasure to her beauty-seeing eye; and over its lovely waters the richly toned Cathedral chimes, and the bugle note from the barracks, tell the time of day, and ring out calls to worship to-day, just as they did when she lived in this house on its banks. This view she constantly enjoyed while they lived in that river house, — looking down the river from the porch, — and she refers to its loveliness in her letters.

Along this river bank of a Sunday evening the soldier and his lass stroll to-day, with utter unconcern for the passing beholder, as they did then, making picturesque bits of red coat and white gown against the blue river-line, — the red of coat seeming to be compelled to keep the rules of true picture-making by carrying a line of the red across a certain narrow place on the white.

It is just the same to-day; and seemingly the very same children play under the willows, with

VIEW OF THE RIVER FROM PORCH OF "KEKA BOM."

their dog friends, and drive cows leisurely along
early in the morning and late at night.

Mrs. Ewing had another home on the bank of
the St. John — much farther "down river" (as they

RUINS OF OLD ROSE HALL, WHERE BENEDICT ARNOLD ONCE LIVED
AND MRS. EWING STAYED.

say) than " Reka Dom." There she occupied the
large drawing-room in an interesting old house
known as " Rose Hall," and noted for its lovely
river view and the fine old trees about its

grounds. This place is of historic interest also, for it was there that the traitor Benedict Arnold lived while in Canada. A pile of ruins is now all that is left of the place (which was destroyed by fire years ago). Here once was heard the martial tread of this mysterious man as he walked up and down in meditation bent, and here our little lady trod the trees and flowers among; here the weeds pathetically wave over the crumbled hearth-stones, and the cows graze all about, while birds undisturbed build in the trees overhead, and countless crickets chirp their everlasting note of the " unchangeable " under all the seeming change of this busy world.

CHAPTER II.

MANY an amusing anecdote is recalled of the industry and dauntless energy of this "little body with the great heart" (as her sister tells us she is described by a friend) who desired to do all things.

A story is told of one of the houses she occupied having such an offensive wall paper as to offend her artistic eye; and on her complaining of it to a Canadian visitor, this latter said, half in fun, that of course a Canadian girl would be able to get over the difficulty by papering the room herself, but she supposed an English girl would not know how, as, in her opinion, "English girls had only two left hands and no head."

This at once caused our little lady, and her friend Mrs. Medley, to resent the implied discredit

to the Old World training of a girl, and they at
once resolved to show what an " English girl " could
do if her powers were put to the test.

She accordingly bought " a delicate, useless, lav-
ender-tinted wall paper " (as I was told), and
though she did not probably know the difference
between a " hanger " and a whitewash brush, she
nevertheless proceeded to put up that paper. Of
this paper-hanging she gives such a bright account
in a letter — that of Oct. 12, 1868 — that one has
the whole picture. But she does not add what was
told to me by an onlooker — (in fact, the very caller
whose remarks upon English girls called forth the
event) — that while the two intrepid ladies were
hurrying up their work, to have it done when
Major Ewing should come home, he suddenly and
unexpectedly appeared. At his emphatic exclama-
tion of amazement, on seeing them on tall ladders
wielding brushes in such a professional manner, his
little wife, who had just finished what she consid-
ered her greatest achievement on that wall, — the
pasting over the chimney, — was overcome by her
laughter. Standing on the mantlepiece as she was,

she had to bend forward to recover her balance, and leaning against that "lovely" paper, left the print of a pasty apron and hands in the very centre! The house is little changed, but oh, that that print of apron and hands could now be seen over the hearth-stone!

CHAPTER III.

MAJOR Ewing had his office in a small red brick building joining the old gray barracks now occupied by the officers and their families.

The drawing opposite shows some parts of this picturesque barrack as it is to-day, with bits of its unique life.

The children still play with the regimental dogs as they did in days of old, and here Mrs. Ewing used to come to sit under the great old willows, whence she could get those lovely glimpses of the blue river beyond.

It was in this very yard that she saw the pet bear of the regiment eating his dinner, while his favorite dog sat by and "licked his nose every time it came up from the bucket," as she writes in one of her home letters.

THE OLD BARRACKS

EST
1895

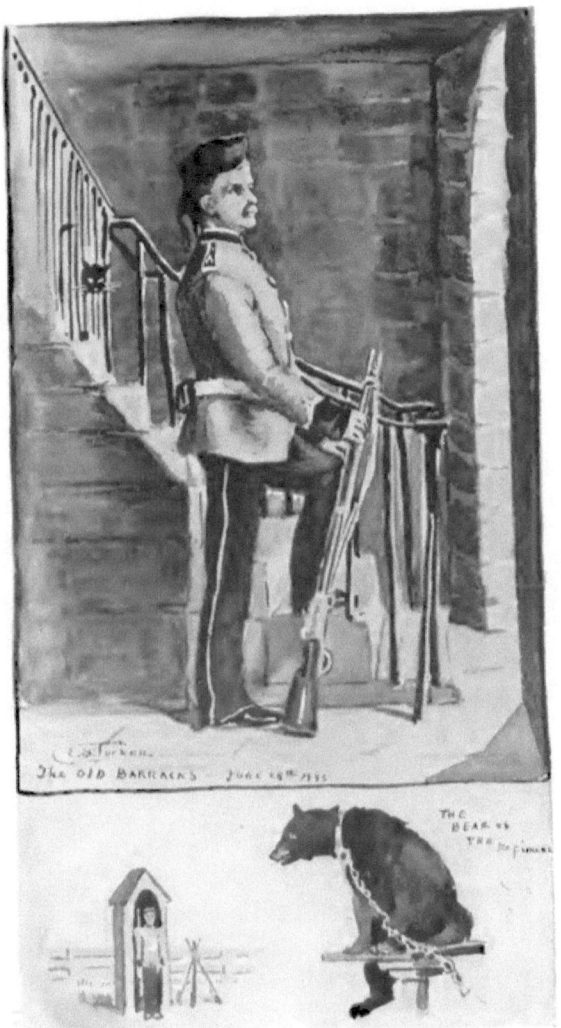

The OLD BARRACKS — JUNE 18th 1895

THE BEAR vs THE REGIMENT

ON GUARD.

Here one may see, as in her day, the various scenes of a military life, — a red-coated British soldier, standing "at ease" under the old gallery by the worn stairs with his black cat friend peeping through the rails, or running a lawn-mower over the well-kept tennis green.

It was in these barracks that she found and rescued a black retriever from death, he having been shut up and basely deserted by the outgoing regiment. She named him Trouvè, and it is his likeness she has drawn in her story of "Benjy in Beastland," as Nox. There is a descendant of Black Trouvè's at the barracks to-day, — the children's pet and playfellow. Poor Trouvè had such an appetite that he was never satisfied, and was always stealing the meat for dinner; and his mistress had often to send and borrow of some kind neighbor, "as company was expected and Trouvè had eaten the joint!"

His mistress's fondness for all animals is shown throughout her writings. In reading that delicious bit of bush-life depicted by Father and Mother Hedgehog in the tale of " Father Hedgehog and his Neighbors," one can see how truly the author saw under prickly coats of quills the true instincts of animal life.

Dogs were her special favorites, and nothing was too good for them to eat, and no place too clean to be climbed on by their muddy paws. She was always most tender of hurting their feelings, while many a stray pussy has found a comfortable home with her.

She did not care to cage a bird, for she loved them too deeply, — as she has shown in her " Idyll of a Wood."

Her dear dogs were her intimate friends, and once when she was calling at the house of a friend, where the vestibule had been newly scrubbed scrupulously clean, she was asked by her hostess to leave her dog, whose feet and coat were very muddy, out on the steps. She did so, but was compelled to go out several times during

her visit, and whisper words of apology and con-
dolence in the ear of her big banished pet, for
fear he might be hurt in his doggish mind — at
being left outside.

Here is another instance of her tender, droll
ways with her dog friends.

A visitor calling at her house one day found
her deep in writing, every chair and table being full
of papers and books, so that there was no room
for the tea-tray when the servant brought it in.
Mrs. Ewing, looking up, said, "Oh, put it on the
floor." So down it went. Now one of the dog
friends (a great fellow) was present, and of course
was curious to sniff the contents of the tray. The
visitor was horrified at seeing his great muzzle
nosing over the things, and exclaimed about it.
Down on the floor beside him went his tender
mistress, and with both arms about his neck she
whispered to him not to mind that "horrid per-
son's" insinuations and suspicions, but to watch
her, that when she went she did not "carry away
the silver spoons with her!" Wherever she went
her dear dogs went with her, and wherever she

speaks of animal life in her books, she shows her deep interest in their welfare, and insight into their habits.

MRS. EWING AND HECTOR.

CHAPTER IV.

ALL of her friends remember Mrs. Ewing's keen appreciation of anything humorous, and the ready names, both apt and droll, but always quite inoffensive, that she applied to people and things as her vivid imagination suggested.

Even in the choir of the Cathedral, where she always wished to be most reverent, her sense of the ridiculous sometimes overcame her, and she would have to smile almost audibly at some little incident insignificant in itself.

Across from where she sat in the choir of the church, she could see the verger blowing the bellows of the great organ, and as his stooping figure bent over, the long handle of the bellows stuck out from under the drooping fold of his black robe, giving the droll appearance of a tail!

3

This was always, to her imagination, a most comical sight, and more than once she smiled at her friend on the seat opposite, quite upsetting that quiet lady's dignity.

One little lady in the choir, who always slid and glided into her seat with an undulating movement, never allowing her garments to touch anything as she went, was called by her, " Patha Furtiva," which is the Hebrew for a " thing which glides." Another's voice she always spoke of as " weepingly pitched " — which perfectly described it !

There was a family of unruly children living near her, by whose actions she was always much entertained. Doubtless some of the rather naughty — but oh, so natural! — boys and girls in some of her stories are drawn from these very children's characters.

On one occasion, when she was calling on their mother, sitting in the parlor, they noticed a rustling or scrambling in the great fireplace, behind the old fashioned fire-board. Presently down came this board flat, with a puff of dust, disclos-

MRS. EWING'S SEAT IN CHOIR OF CATHEDRAL.

ing all the children in a bunch, with sooty faces
and garments, *sitting in the fireplace!* They had
hidden there, but, quarrelling, had pushed the
board down.

Mrs. Ewing was interested in a story, then
coming out in "Aunt Judy's Magazine," called
"The Scaramouches," and she then and there
bestowed upon these "mischief makers" the ap-
propriate title of Scaramouches, by which they
were always known thereafter.

She was interested in all the customs of this
quaint colonial town, and of the Canadian winter
dress she speaks in the story of "Three Christmas-Trees," where a boy is described as wearing
"a hooded Indian winter coat of blue and scarlet," which is the picturesque Canadian blanket
coat of winter. In that story she speaks also of
the dry cold snow, so strange and wonderful to her
English eyes, telling how, when the boys tried to
make a real live snow-man, "the snow would
not stick anywhere except on his shoulders,"
showing the extreme dryness and powdery light-
ness for which our Canadian snow is noted.

In this story there is an account of the life in this little town of her day, which tells of a custom still kept up by the Governor of the Province, of giving the children a Christmas-tree, or a party some time through the winter. Christmas-trees were then by no means so universal, even in England, as they now are, and in this little colonial town they were unknown, — unknown, that is, till the Governor's wife gave her great children's party.

" The Governor had given a great many parties in his time. He had entertained big wigs and little wigs, the passing military and the local grandees. Everybody who had the remotest claim to attention had been attended to: the ladies had had their full share of balls and pleasure parties: only one class of the population had any complaint to prefer against his hospitality; but the class was a large one — it was the children. However, he was a bachelor, and knew next to nothing about little boys and girls : let us pity rather than blame him. At last he took to himself a wife; and among the many advantages of this important step was a due recognition of the claims of these young

citizens.   It was towards happy Christmas-tide
that 'the Governor's amiable and admired lady'
(as she was styled in the local newspaper) sent invitations for the first children's party.   At the top
of the note-paper was a very red robin, who carried
a blue Christmas greeting in his mouth, and at the
bottom — written with the A. D. C.'s best flourish
— were the magic words, *A Christmas-Tree.*   In
spite of the flourishes — partly, perhaps, because of
them — the A. D. C.'s handwriting, though hand-
some, was rather illegible.   But for all this, most
of the children invited contrived to read these
words, and those who could not do so were not
slow to learn the news by hearsay.   There was to
be a Christmas-tree!   It would be like a birthday
party, with this above ordinary birthdays, that there
were to be presents for every one.

  " One of the children invited lived in a little white
house, with a spruce fir-tree before the door.   The
spruce fir did this good service to the little house,
that it helped people to find their way to it ; and
it was by no means easy for a stranger to find his
way to any given house in this little town, espe-

cially if the house was small and white, and stood
in one of the back streets.   For most of the houses
were small, and most of them were painted white,
and the back streets ran parallel with each other,
and had no names, and were all so much alike that
it was very confusing.   For instance, if you had
asked the way to Mr. So-and-So's, it is very probable that some friend would have directed you as
follows: 'Go straight forward and take the first
turning to your left, and you will find that there
are four streets, which run at right angles to the
one you are in and parallel with each other.   Each
of them has got a big pine in it — one of the old
forest trees.   Take the last street but one, and the
fifth white house you come to is Mr. So-and-So's.
He has green blinds and a colored servant.'   You
would not always have got such clear directions as
these, but with them you would probably have
found the house at last, partly by accident, partly
by the blinds and colored servant.   Some of the
neighbors affirmed that the little white house had
a name; that all the houses and streets had names,
only they were traditional and not recorded any-

where; that very few people knew them, and no-
body made any use of them. The name of the
little white house was said to be Trafalgar Villa,
which seemed so inappropriate to the modest
peaceful little home, that the man who lived in it
tried to find out why it had been so called. He
thought that his predecessor must have been in
the navy, until he found that he had been the
owner of what is called a ' dry-goods store,' which
seems to mean a shop where things are sold which
are not good to eat or drink — such as drapery.
At last somebody said, that as there was a public-
house called 'The Duke of Wellington' at the corner of the street, there probably had been a nearer
one called ' The Nelson,' which had been burnt
down, and that the man who built ' The Nelson '
had built the house with a spruce fir before it, and
that so the name had arisen, — an explanation
which was just so far probable, that public-houses
and fires were of frequent occurrence in those parts."

This was the way it was when she was living
here. How fond she was of the beautiful woods,
and of always searching for, and finding the small-

est thing, seeing the fulness of God's great love in
all, and so, keenly appreciating it.

See how in her " Idyll of the Wood " she makes
the wise old man say: " Well, well, my children,
 to know and love a
wood truly, it may be
that one must live in
it as I have done;
and then a lifetime
will scarcely reveal
all its beauties or ex-
haust its lessons; but
even then one must have eyes that see, and ears
that hear, or one misses a good deal," — speaking all through this delightsome Idyll as only
one who knows and sees the " woods " root and
branch can speak of its glories.   I seem to feel her
very presence in those woods to-day, and love to
fancy her eager face peering among the waving
ferns for the hidden treasures, and looking up
through the thick, waving branches laced into a
canopy overhead, now in deep shade and now
flecked over with the peeping sunshine.

CHAPTER V.

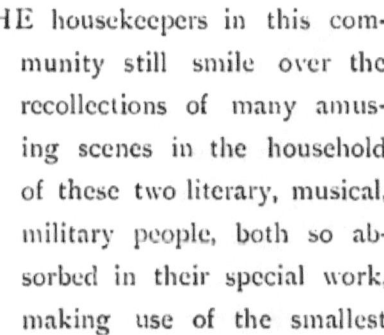

THE housekeepers in this community still smile over the recollections of many amusing scenes in the household of these two literary, musical, military people, both so absorbed in their special work, making use of the smallest amount of furniture possible, and allowing the household to " run itself," as the saying is. Funny times and droll mistakes are recalled, such as the stopping of a stove-pipe hole in the chimney with a bath sponge, causing a long search for this article, and a smoking flue in consequence of the stopped draught, windows being left wide to let in winter breezes and do away with the smoke, while the occupant of the room sat wrapped up and complained of the cold!

Many a morning, early, the pair used to go over to Bishopscote and beg to be asked to breakfast, as that meal had not been provided for in their household.

However, with the most, at times, untidy aspect of rooms, it was always a very attractive place to visit, and many loved to go to this home with its nameless charm of literary disorder, always some pretty decorations, and here and there Mrs. Ewing's own sketches pinned on the walls.

Ah, it was the gentle manner of the beautiful hostess, — that inborn grace of spirit which in a short conversation would cause the most critical housekeeper to entirely forget the surroundings, and to rejoice in that sweet society! A visitor would perhaps find her hostess seated on the hearth-rug, her papers on her lap, feet outstretched, writing away to get her manuscript complete for the story that was to go by the English mail, an orderly standing the while, like a wooden sentinel, waiting to take the packet when it should be ready.

Waving her pen hospitably, and going straight

THE WINDOW OF THE ROOM
IN WHICH "REKA DOM" WAS WRITTEN

WINDOW IN "REKA DOM."

on with her work, she would invite the friend
to enter — to excuse the disorder and lack of
chairs (all occupied by piles of manuscript), sug-
gesting that if the caller really wished to help
her, she could do so by gathering up the various
piles in the order of their numbering, and bring
them to her to tie up.

At one time this little mistress, so absorbed in
her great work that all else seemed of minor
importance (for which *we* ought to be truly thankful), determined to give a dinner party in return
for the many invitations and hospitalities that
she had received.   So many obstacles, in the
way of lack of proper dishes and the necessary
accoutrements for such an affair, in her limited
military establishment, arose, that they would have
daunted many a housewife, — but not our little lady
of the "great heart."   Her ready wit supplied the
lack, and her own generous and liberal mind made
her believe that others were the same ; so she sent
out and borrowed all the necessary articles, in-
cluding glass, china, and silver candlesticks, from
her neighbors and friends.

4

Her rooms were crowded, and it was a most brilliant affair — where the people, with appreciation of her entertainment, noticed but little the lack of things which usually go to make up the substance of social affairs. As the last guests were leaving, however, there was a great uproar heard from the basement kitchen regions of the house, which became so pronounced that Mrs. Ewing asked her husband to descend and inquire into the cause thereof, as she feared the orderly and the borrowed butler were quarrelling. He found this indeed the case, as the two were having a stand-up fight amid the wreck of many borrowed articles of glass, dropped in his heat by the butler, on the kitchen floor, while the cook was prone upon the hearth in a semi-intoxicated state, and literally a " heap of smoking ruins " (as Mrs. Ewing expressed it), having put a lighted pipe into her pocket ·

Her merriment over this amusing incident was (as always) most infectious, and what to some would have been a trial and almost a disgrace, was turned into an amusing episode, looked

at with her full appreciation of its humorous
aspect.

Her absorption in anything which gave her an
idea for a story was really wonderful, and showed how
her active mind was always in its beloved work.

Once when she was calling at Bishopscote, the
English mail, arriving then only once or twice a
month, came, bringing to the Bishop a new book
of interesting travel and research in the Arctic
Seas. She seized upon the volume and sat down
to devour its contents, which suggested a new
theme to her. When it came time to leave she
refused to be torn away from her treasure trove,
and begged hard to be invited to "stay to tea,"
that she might finish the book. But this not
being at all possible in the Bishop's household
that special evening, she was compelled to part
with it, and going home, at once wrote out the
story it inspired, which afterward developed into
that charming tale of Kerguslen's Land, with such
a charming description of the home of the mysterious albatross, and the fascinating conversations
carried on between Father and Mother Albatross,

over their nest of little ones, about the cast-away man, — Father Albatross discoursing about him in this fashion, in superior contempt: —

" They are very curious creatures " (he says to Mother A.). " The fancy they have for wandering about between sea and sky when nature has not enabled them to support themselves in either, is truly wonderful! "

The whole dialogue is most delightful, showing her marvellous insight throughout this, as in all her other wonderful animal stories, both of birds and furry folk. She would forget all else in reading a book, and become wrapped in a dream of reproducing an idea suggested by some subject in it. How keenly she saw from a child's eyes, and with a child's mind its outlook on life, is shown by the " real child " language in those stories where the child hero or heroine are made to, as it were, tell the story themselves; " Mary's Meadow" and " Flat-Iron for a Farthing " being especially good examples of this wonderful power of hers, of being able to see from all points.

Here is another sweet recollection: While Mrs.

MRS. EWING TELLING STORIES TO THE CHILDREN.

Ewing was living here, a little lad was very ill, and kept within doors all winter. Our tender little lady used to go every evening, towards dusk ("story time"), and tell to him the most beautiful stories by firelight.

This "story-telling" was a great gift of hers, as her sister relates in her account of her childhood. And the stories were so wonderful, and, told in her own sweet manner, so irresistible, that a group of grown folks usually crowded about the door of the room where she was "telling a story" to that favored little boy!

Her lessons to her class in Sunday School were made so attractive that the class next to hers had hard work not to neglect their own lessons and teacher in listening to her most interesting way of putting things.

CHAPTER VI.

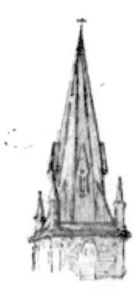

THE Cathedral of Fredericton was a great source of comfort and pleasure to Mrs. Ewing, who was always devoted to her church, and did not expect to find so beautiful a specimen architecturally of an English church in our Canadian land.

Her husband was organist in this choir during their stay, and wrote many beautiful musical compositions during his lifetime, perhaps the best known being that grand hymn "Jerusalem the Golden," which has sometimes been wrongly attributed to his uncle, Bishop Ewing.[1] He also conducted the Choral Society, of which she speaks

[1] Major Alexander Ewing passed away in the summer of 1895, and in the interesting account of his life, printed at the time in the "Aberdeen Times," there is special mention made of his wonderful musical abilities.

in her letters.   How dearly she loved to sit in her
seat in that choir, listening to the inspired tones
from her beloved husband's hands, under her
revered Bishop, and opposite to her friend his
wife !

Sometimes to-day, when one sees this latter
gentle lady sitting in her accustomed place in the
choir, one can fancy that the scene before her
fades away, leaving but the two faces she loved so
well, — that of " her dear Lord " in his Bishop's seat,
and of the sweet singer opposite to her.   For, as
this singer herself says, in " The Story of a Short
Life," " Can the last parting do much to hurt such
friendships between good souls, who have so long
learnt to say farewell ; to love in absence, to trust
through silence, and to have faith in reunion ? "
Surely, blessed are such reunions !

In this seat in the choir did our little lady love
to sit, much enjoying always the beauty of the
Cathedral with its many rich parts, each having
its own special meaning in ornament, in window,
and in the very shape of the building itself, all
bearing witness to the deep thought and reverent

CATHEDRAL OF FREDERICTON.

care bestowed upon its structure by him who was its first Bishop, who for so many years devoted his life to its erection. The rich chime of bells, and much of the ornamentation, were brought over by his efforts from England, and in the shadow of its beautiful spire his body rests to-day, close under its gray walls, which are a fitting memorial to his love and zeal for his church and its people.

There she must often have watched, as we can to-day, the red coats of the officers as they filed up the centre aisle of the church, with much clanking of swords and ringing of spurred heels. And out of the beautiful Eastern Door she has looked in loving admiration, seeing through its stone Gothic curves, in the soft light of a summer evening, the arches of the graceful branching trees over the path beyond. As I sketched this seat of hers, the verger handed me an anthem composed by Major Ewing, with this, to me at that time, singularly meaning-full title, " Why seek ye the living among the dead?" which seemed so to fit her own hopeful views of death.

In many of Mrs. Ewing's clever sketches about Fredericton the old gray willows appear. She used to form merry parties of sketchers, herself always ready to help and offer assistance to unaccustomed hands.

The spire of her beloved Cathedral is also often seen, taken from all points of view; and much of her time was spent within the hospitable, vine-covered walls of Bishopscote, — of which we have a little picture, with a glimpse of its gentle minister's wife in the doorway, to whose aid we owe so many of these recollections.

Here she always made herself quite at home, — running in and out at all times, finding in the Bishop's wife a loving friend and admonisher, though the latter must often have been sorely tried by our little lady's caprices and unpractical experiments.

Like a child, her bright, joyous nature seized upon any novel experience with pleasure, and any play was entered into with zest.

Once in the attic she discovered an old set of battledore and shuttlecock, and soon had every one in a merry game. And to-day, there may be

EASTERN DOOR OF THE CATHEDRAL.

seen, in testimony of her eager play, a broken
battledore belonging to the old set!

BISHOPSCOTE.

Her love of doing everything, whether she
understood the mechanical part of it or not, was
shown once when she came to Bishopscote, and,
finding every one busily engaged on some work
for church decoration, she determined to work with
them, and insisted that she should be allowed to
do so. Thereupon she proceeded to cut out the

letters for an illuminated text, — from the only
paper obtainable for it, — but cut them *every one
out on the wrong side of the paper*, so that
upon turning them all were backward! She
crushed them up in her hands and declared all
would be right, for she would send to England
for more paper; but upon being told how impos-
sible this would be, as the work had to be ready
for the morrow, her contrition was great! Down
upon her knees she went, with her hands in a
prayerful attitude before her, and, supplicating
them all to forgive her for her naughtiness, drove
away the cloud caused by her mischievousness,
with her droll merry manners, as was always
her way of doing, from a child.

Her love of fun was so irresistible, her repent-
ance for wrong-doing so great, the sternest heart
could not hold anything against her. Many a
scrape has she got her beloved doggies out of,
by her manner of turning away the wrath of their
accusers; for the love she bore these dogs, great
and small, was wonderful.

MY MRS. OVER-THE-WAY
IN HER DOOR

CHAPTER VII.

BACK of the town there is a range of low hills, and on that part of it to which the University of New Brunswick has given the name of College Road, she used to walk and enjoy its Canadian aspect. It was from that point many of her lovely sketches in color were painted. Here, also, in the winter, she and her husband, with their dear friends the Misses R —— and others, used to walk on snow-shoes, and sit under shelters made of fir boughs, going over their Hebrew study together, or singing with their keen love for music. The Ewings greatly enjoyed the "musical evenings" (of which she speaks in one of the letters printed here) spent with these friends while in Fredericton.

In her walks over these hills, and in the gardens of the town, she found many new flower friends.

The Trillium she first saw here, and it was a great joy to her, with its beauty and grace. After returning to England she had some seeds of this plant sent out to her, and tried to grow it there, and it inspired her to write the beautiful legend of " The Trinity Flower," in which she immortalizes this pure blossom of our wilds, thus describing its beauty : " Every part was threefold. The leaves were three, the petals three, the sepals three. The flower was snow white, but on each of the three parts it was shaded with crimson stripes, like white garments dyed in blood."

The Lily of the Valley was another special favorite of hers, and inspired the graceful legend which she wrote, wherein she calls the plant " Ladders to Heaven," saying, " It hath a rare and delicate perfume, and having many white bells on many footstalks up the stem, one above the other, as the angels stood in Jacob's dream, the common children call it ' Ladders to Heaven.' "

She found so many new wild flowers, that she

FIR BOUGH SHELTER.

made an extensive collection, of which she speaks
in one letter, and I am told that she also added the
Mellicite Indian names to her specimens, through
the aid of her Indian "brother" of whom she speaks,

MRS. EWING'S BARN AND CANOE.

Peter Poultice, who came from his encampment
(there to-day) just across the river to visit his interested friends, the pale faces from over the great
ocean, and to sell them bead work and moccasons,
as is the custom of the red brother here always.

They had a canoe from him, and Mrs. Ewing
was remarkably fearless in this frail craft for one
so unaccustomed to such venturous boating. The
temptations to her, of the many beautiful views on

and about this great broad river St. John, and of being able with a canoe to enter the lovely little streams which flow into it, made her enjoy it keenly.

I can fancy her delight in the great beauty of those two streams, the Nash-waak, and the Nash-wa-sis (or little Nashwaak), known to every canoe lover in these parts.

THE OLD NASHWAAK BRIDGE.

This picturesque bridge is the entrance to that lovely little stream the Nashwaak, which she describes in her letter that tells of their picnics in canoes. It was evidently then as it is now, except that the graceful bridge has been replaced

by a hideous structure, which I am glad her artist
eye did not have to see in those days.   And to-day
the sawdust from the great ruthless mill at the
head of the stream is fast filling up and spoiling
the beautiful wavy stream, narrowing it even to the
exclusion of canoes.

CHAPTER VIII.

ER great fondness for flowers is seen all through her writings, and her "Letters from a Little Garden" shows her practical experience in flower growing and tending. In her books she gives good advice to other flower lovers, quoting from Charles Dudley Warner's "My Summer in a Garden," with a full appreciation of its delicious humor.

In her verses and maxims for use in gardening ("Garden Lore"), two trite maxims bespeak the thorough sympathy she had for plants and plant growers. She says, in this "Garden Lore," "Cut a rose for your neighbor, and it will tell two buds to blossom for you;" and again: "Enough comes out of anybody's old garden in autumn to stock a new one for somebody else. But you want

sympathy on one side, and sense on the other, and
they are rarer than most perennials!"

How sorely tried such a lover of plants and
"little gardens" must have been in her life as
an officer's wife, sent from post to post, at having
to break up her homes, leaving many little gardens
just started!

How tenderly, in the letter written from Aldershot Camp back to Fredericton, shortly after she
returned to England, does she speak of her house
plants there, and the care she takes of them!   She
was very fond of the dear old English custom of
having house mottoes; and the one reproduced in
the front of this book she had painted and framed,
to hang on the wall of each new home: —

> " *Ut migraturus, habita.*"
> " Dwell as if about to depart!"

Another favorite one of her many house mottoes
is this cleverly arranged Latin one, curtailing one
word into four meanings: —

> " *Amore, more, ore, re.*"
> " By love, by manners, by word, by action!"

Things with meanings rejoiced her heart, and her own sweet namesake flower, the Chinese Primrose, which is about her portrait here, was a favorite with her; and it seems to make the little primrose as familiar to us as a choice potted plant, dearer and nearer, to know of its association with her. A spray of this flower is carved upon her quiet tomb at Trull.

This letter was written shortly after her return to England.

Mrs. Ewing's Letter.

25 *Feb.*, 1870.
X LINES S. CAMP, ALDERSHOT.

MY DEAR B——: We were delighted to get yours (and M.'s) long letters. We have many kind correspondents in Fredericton, and all the news interests us. You have had a wonderful winter. Here we have had a little — so cold — that frozen sponges, cruelly killed plants, and cutting winds piercing our wooden walls, quite recalled New Brunswick! . . . I used to take my poor plants into my bedroom at night, and cover them up —

but all in vain; they were frozen as completely
as in D—— J——'s "old barn!"

But oh! I *do* revel in the spring days we get
now from time to time. I *long* to see primroses
—and I have not seen a daisy for three years.
How I hope they won't send us away first to
"furrin" parts! We still know nothing about our
future. We have many charming friends here,
and are very comfortable. Mr. Ewing has a *very*
nice organ to play upon at " All Saints' " near
here. We often go there on Sunday, for he plays
very often at the services, and there is also a
Wednesday evening service at which he always
plays. But we have very few week-day services,
and miss the daily prayer at the Cathedral very
much indeed. If at our next station we have
more "church privileges," it will go far to recon-
cile me to the move. I hope to go home before
we settle again. Indeed, we have promised my
mother to do so if all be well. . . .

We had an evening party the other night in
our tiny habitation! We turned out of our bedroom (which opens into the drawing-room), and

I made a pretty little coffee-room of it. All went
off very well, but it seems dreary work to me to
have a commonplace evening when we have been
used to *musical* ones! I fear we could not get
one up here. And then the rooms are too small.
The dining-room is so narrow that we could only
sit on one side of the supper table. . . .

At the beginning of this month I was very busy
composing valentines for my sisters, etc., etc., and
Rex insisted on having one, so I had to make
one for him, of which Trouvè was the subject!
That dear old boy is very well, and in fine con-
dition. We have another dog also living with
us, and they are great friends. Trouvè sleeps
with us, and the other sleeps with my maid.

Do you know whether the S——s are still in
Fredericton? I have often wondered what be-
came of them in the giving up of the barracks.
They are very unpractical — poor souls — and I
would like to hear if they were doing well or ill.
Can you find out for me, my dear?

We are very glad to hear how the Choral S.
holds on. The other day, we and some friends

of ours went to the Crystal Palace, and heard
Mendelssohn's (Lobgesang). We *did* enjoy it!
One verse of the *choral* was sung *in unison* by all
voices (about two hundred and fifty or more).
Imagine the effect! My husband's love and mine.
Trouvè's respects to *Thistle.*

Yours, dear B——, *very affectionately,*

JULIANA HORATIA EWING.

How like her own dear
self is this rare plant,
coming from a far-
away land, but famil-
iarizing itself
to us so sweetly
in an every-day

life, until now it is a household favorite! It is not
hard to understand the deep hold she obtained on

the hearts of her Canadian friends, in the all too
short years she spent with us, on this continent.
And now, comes a budget of her own brilliant
letters which we are indeed fortunate in secur-
ing, full of a sweet personality and gayety — in
whose glowing pages we can see more clearly
into the character and life of our dear friend than
in any other way now possible to us. They are
indeed a rich treat, and cannot fail to reawaken
our love for her, and to help towards keeping
that sweet memory "green" in our hearts. In
fact, the sketches and letters taken together seem
to be an autobiography almost, written and illustrated by herself, of her life with us.

MAJOR AND MRS. EWING AND HECTOR.

MRS. EWING'S LETTERS

AND

FAC-SIMILES OF HER WATER-COLOR SKETCHES

MADE WHILE IN FREDERICTON.

Mrs. Ewing's Letters.

———•———

FREDERICTON, NEW BRUNSWICK,
July, 1867.

MY DEAR MRS. EWING, — . . . Since we must
be "abroad" somewhere, I do not think we could
well have been more fortunate in a station than
we are in being sent here. There is that most
disagreeable Atlantic between us and Great Bri-
tain, but otherwise it is in many respects very
like home. We hear rather appalling accounts
of the winter, but we were told awful things of the
summer heats; and yet (except for occasional op-
pressive days) we have found it delightful. It is
rather blazing in the morning often, and makes
one rather giddy if one attempts to walk much;
but the evenings and nights are delicious, and
quite cool. Fredericton is on the river, and all

by the river side it is lovely, and we have not yet
been able to decide by what lights and at what
time of day it looks most beautiful. Very fine
willows grow on the bank, and the fireflies float
about under them like falling stars. The moonlight and starlight nights are splendid, and the
skies are particularly beautiful. We were detained
for some days both at Halifax and at S. John;
but we are very glad that our lot has fallen here
rather than in either of those places. Halifax has
lovely country near it, but S. John is a *town* pure
and simple; and I think if one must live in a
town one likes it to be as highly civilized a city
as possible. S. John is more like a watering
place without the shore. I suppose the New
Brunswickers would be duly indignant at my not
calling Fredericton a town, for it is a CITY! but it
is all in lovely country, the streets are planted with
trees, and have no names, and there are *very* few
lamps; most of them are like shady lanes, with
pretty wooden houses with (generally) very pretty
faces at the windows! For another attraction
which this place possesses is the beauty of the

women, both of the upper and lower classes. Not
that we have seen any one *very* beautiful woman
(such as one sometimes sees at home) but that,
almost every girl you meet is very *pretty*, and very
gentle and sweet looking. The young ladies have
particularly pleasant, unaffected manners, too. . . .

The ferns, flowers, mosses, and lichens in the
woods about here are most beautiful, and it is an
utterly new pleasure to me to find so many plants
I have never seen. In fact, the botany of these
parts seems richly luxuriant, and to have been
very little investigated. I have dried a few things
in my blotting-books, etc., but we have no appara-
tus with us. However, we have ordered two
boards at the carpenter's for a press, and when
we have out a box from England we shall have
some proper paper and portfolio sent — and I hope
we shall be able to bring home some specimens
of the beautiful things out here. For want of
proper means to preserve those we first got, I
have been making rough coloured sketches of
them in a note-book of Alexander's which we have
devoted to the purpose ; and whenever we meet

anybody who seems likely to be knowing on the
subject, we ask the names of the flowers. Some
have exquisite perfumes, which, unhappily, one can
neither figure nor preserve! One almost wonders
that more plants from this country are not culti-
vated in England, as whatever can stand these
winters would well live with us. We have just
heard of some wonderful orchids in a bog two or
three miles away, and I am greatly impatient to
get at them, for vegetation is so rapid here, — the
flowers are out and then gone in a day or two. . . .

I am sending you a small sketch of our house,
and also one from a hasty sketch I made in my
note-book as we came up the river into Fredericton. It was, in fact, our first view of our new
home. . . . You cannot think how lovely it is
coming up the river from S. John to this place.
The colouring is so exquisite, the sky and clouds
are so beautiful, the pine woods look at times the
richest purple in the distance; and the foliage of
the white birches, and brushwood, and grass near
the shore, was of most vivid pale greens when
we came up. I suppose in autumn, when the

maple trees turn scarlet, it will be lovelier still.
People say that whatever you may have heard or
read about American woods in autumn, nothing
but seeing them can give you an idea of the
wonderful brilliancy of their colours. . . .

I must tell you about our house. You will, I
think, be amused at its *palatial* appearance; it *is*
much larger than necessary, though Rex justly
says I always give it a more magnificent appearance on paper than it really possesses. It *has*,
however, twenty-one rooms in it!! though they
are not very large ones. He *could* keep an hotel
— or invite my seven brothers and sisters to visit
me. We talk of giving *Trot* (the dog) a bedroom, sitting-room (and he *might* have a dressing-
room!) to himself when he arrives. Don't think
us quite mad! We had much humbler inten-
tions, but it fell out thus: When we arrived we
were told we should have to wait a long time for
a house, as none were vacant; of course it was
desirable to get one as soon as possible. The
second day, Rex discovered this one, which was
in a fearful state of disrepair, but was being put

in order by the landlord: he took it, and we are only furnishing just what we want. It has many great advantages. It is in the best situation we could have chosen, there is a well of good water, we have very nice neighbours, and we are close to the Cathedral. We are not overlooked, and have a lovely lookout over the river, with a ferry-boat just opposite to our front door. There is ample space for a good garden, and our landlord is building us a huge sort of barn, which I fancy is to embrace coach-house, stables etc., and which (as we possess no equipage) I think will have to be devoted to the .... we purpose to keep: he will consequently have as much spare space as ourselves! Fancy Alexander coming in yesterday and announcing to me his intention (please the pigs!) of fattening a porker for Christmas!! An officer has told him that a young pig may be bought for half a dollar, and live on the household refuse till Christmas, and then either be killed or sold. As we neither of us like pork, I think our "little pig will go to market!" Most opportunely .... turning out his (very untidy)

drawers yesterday he found a half dollar which
had been there since he was in China, so we may
look upon the pig as purchased — so to speak.

August 1st. 1867.   "Reka Dom."
Fredericton. N. B.

MY DEAREST FATHER, — I am going to write to
you this time. . . . We have had some very rainy
weather, and some *intensely* hot (even Rex allowing that it *was* overpowering and like China).
To-day, a cloudless sky and brilliant sun, but a
refreshing breeze; and what breeze is to be got,
we get. — living by the river. Did I tell mother
of that beautiful thunder-storm we saw just before
leaving our last hotel? The sky had been of
such a blue as I never saw, — a pure, intense,
opaque, *speedwell* colour. It seems a poor compari-
son, but it reminded me of the blue which they
use on church or cathedral roofs with golden
stars, and which is usually deeper and more intense
than the sky which it represents. On this were
wonderful cumulus clouds of splendid tints.
One grand mass standing off in *awfully* powerful

relief, against a golden glow, reminded us of
Sinai, when the mount burned with fire, and
one expected to see the tables of the law appear.
These mountainous masses faded after sunset,
and then two other currents of very electrical
appearance touched each other, and till dark
we watched them emitting the loveliest lightning
I ever saw. The sheet lightning was incessant,
and the forked ran among it and cleft the clouds
in the most lovely way. They had a ludicrous
resemblance to two gigantic and wonderful *fire-
stones* perpetually rubbed together. Rex fetched
me to see this storm from the other side of the
house, where I was frantically splashing paint
on to paper, trying to catch the sunset sky,
against which stood off one of the houses they
build here for the swallows. . . .

Last Thursday we went to dine at Government
House, the first time, — about twenty-two people, —
and as we were in the very worst of our difficulties
a capital dinner was an absolute treat! The general introduced me to the Bishop, and he took
me in to dinner. I enjoyed it immensely, for

he is very clever and awfully amusing, and told
me the funniest anecdotes. He has been away
until now, but next day he and Mrs. Medley
called on us, and we like them both extremely.
Mrs. Medley told us some clergyman has been
raving in their house about mother's writings,
and had said that whole pieces were taken out
of Aunt Judy's Magazine into American news-
papers, sometimes without an acknowledgment.
When he went away, the Bishop looked at me
in his point-blank way and said, very kindly, after
his rather awkward fashion, "If you would like
to see Maryland Church, I will drive you there, —
not to-morrow, Saturday is a busy day with me,
but next week." Is n't it kind? So I expect we
shall probably get to see some of the country in
very good company. Yesterday he preached both
A. M. and P. M., and I really doubt if any of our
English swells beat him, on the whole. The learn-
ing, the logic, the irrepressible irony at times, the
intense simplicity, and the exquisite touches of
pathos, I hardly think Oxon, Vaughan, Eber, or
anybody could excel. He preached A. M. on the

" whole creation groaning," etc., and brought out
a forcible and (to me) new idea, — that if we had
been alive in any of the periods of great " disturbance " of the physical world (the glacial or vol-
canic, etc.), our faith would probably have failed
to foresee the physical beauty and order that
would come out of it all: the rocks on the
sunny hillside, the waters in their own places,
the flowers, etc., etc.; and that, although the divi-
sions of the Church of Christ, the distractions and
confusions and inconsistencies which make Chris-
tianity seem almost useless, the darkness of dis-
pensations and all the disturbance of the moral
world, make one inclined to give up hope, we
were to draw comfort from creation. He had
been charmingly sarcastic in the hastiness and
almost invariable erroneousness of man's very
self-satisfied judgment of providence in all times;
but there was a sort of grave authority that was
very impressive as he admonished us that since
God had loved His lower creation so well as to
bring such beautiful order out of such ghastly
confusion, He *would* bring out of all the moral

disorder and disturbance a new heaven and a new
earth for those whom Jesus died to redeem.
Towards the end he gave a practical turn, and
speaking of the love of Christ, — " a love such as
no earthly friend can feel for us, suffering as no
earthly friend ever suffered for one, interced-
ing as no earthly friend *can* plead, a Home at
last such as no one who loves us can provide
here, however they may wish and try." He uses
very simple, forcible language, has a voice as
soft as Vaughan's, and it is as clear as a bell.
He hardly ever lifts his eyes, and uses no action
whatever. His premises and deductions, his biting
bits of sarcasm, and his touches of pathos go down
the Cathedral without the slightest assistance from
"delivery;" but they are just the reverse of the
style of sermon which Goulburn calls "like the
arrow shot at a venture that hit King Ahab,"
with the difference that they seldom hit anybody
in particular. When he is most severe he looks
so awfully innocent. P. M. he preached on Rizpah,
the daughter of Aiah, and the execution of Saul's
sons. It was cleverer than the other, — one of the
ablest bits of Biblical criticism one ever heard.

Rex said the composition seemed to him so perfect.   It really is a wonderful piece of good fortune
to be under him.   He has been out here twenty-
two years (or more, — I forget), and he turns up
at the 7.30 A. M. daily services, and walks into the
Cathedral with a pastoral staff much bigger than
himself.   Tell Regie I have got a "relic" for him
which I will send him.   It is a bit of lichen from
the nameless grave of one of the first settlers here.
In old Judge Parker's garden (a very pretty place,
with a lovely peep of the river through trees, like
an Italian lake), in a field, are the graves of the
first settlers.   On one are some rudely cut initials,
the last being "B."   It was really an affecting
sight, amid the prosperity to which this lovely
spot has attained.   One imagines how beautiful
it must have looked to their eyes as a spot to
"settle" in.   We have made out a great many
both of the ferns and flowers, and we have a good
many in press, and to-day I am going to try and
get some paper to "fix" them in. . . .

> Ever, my dearest Father,
> Your loving daughter,
> J. H. EWING.

11TH SUNDAY AFTER TRINITY, 1867.

WE have the most charming room, with two
windows looking east to the river; Rex says the
view beats the Lake Hotel at Killarney! He
wakes at unearthly hours, and lies wrapt in the
enjoyment of using a telescope in bed!! He kept
us awake from 3 A. M. the first morning, looking
at the view, and indeed it was lovely, — the white
mist rolling off the river, sunrise behind the pine
woods and willows, and canoes coming down
reminding one of Hiawatha's " Like a yellow leaf
it floated." They *do* look just like autumn leaves
floating on the water. I don't think Rex will
exist long without one! . . .

Last Friday we were asked to Government House
for a picnic. . . . We went across the river, and by
water up the Nashwaak Cis. (i. e., Little Nashwaak),
and landed at a very pretty spot, where we ate
luncheon off such lovely old china I wonder his
Excellency had the heart to risk it at a picnic!
The A. D. C. lent Rex his own boat, that Rex
might row me there. I told him I must have a

good wrap and got a buffalo robe to keep me warm,
and sat like a queen in the stern. There were lots
of canoes and a few boats. . . Coming back down
the Cis it was lovely, half dark, and the canoes
gliding past among the shadows. The Cis was
very narrow and required careful steering. I got
some new water lilies. When we got into the big
river again, the wind was very high, and it was
nearly dark, and the waves were quite wonderful.
. . the canoes found it tiresome work. There was
a dance afterwards at Government House, but we
left in good time, and walked home. About half-
past one, I was roused by Rex asking if anything
was the matter. I could hear nothing, but he exclaimed, " It 's the *fire-bell !* " and jumped up like a
shot.

[I must tell you that, the day the Medleys left,
the Bishop told us that he had told his next-door
neighbour where the church plate was, in case of
a fire, and what he specially wished to be saved,
adding that the man had looked at a long box and
said : " Is this valuable ? " " Very," said the Bishop,
" What is it ? *Music ?* " on which, as the Bishop

THE NASHWAAK.

said he did not seem to see it, Rex said, " Well, if
there's a fire, *I* must save the music."]

Well, when I went into the bath-room and saw
the blaze in the sky, it seemed to me to come from
the Medleys, so I told Rex. " Then I must save
the anthems!" he cried in a thunderous voice (it
was almost amusing), and off he went. We
could n't find matches, so he dressed in the dark,
and in the dark I was left. I could hear the
peculiar *roar* of the fire, and see the flames rising
up through the open window. I got awfully
lonely, so I awoke "Sarah" with much difficulty and
got a light, and told her to make a fire and get tea
ready for Rex when he returned, and went back to
the window to watch. Time went on, the fire got
larger, and no Rex returned. At last I got so
nervous I wrapped up, left the house, took my
maid with me. and went off to find the fire, — and
Rex! When we got to the Cathedral and Bishopscote happily it was not there, so on we went. Fire
is very delusive at night, and I may as well say it
was in the position of the Bishop's palace, only
about a quarter of a mile or more further up the

town. As we got nearer we seemed to be going
into the blaze of falling sparks, and at last we found
it. We had passed the place an hour or so before!
It was a square called Phœnix Square, and how
many times it has risen from its own ashes I know
not, but the other half of the square was burned
down just before we came, and when Sarah and
I reached the spot, not one stone was left upon
another, or rather not one plank, for it was wood,
of course. But a large building at the corner, — a
brick house, offices, — which had held out sometime,
was in full blaze. It was a wonderful sight. The
flames poured out of the windows, and *licked* round
the walls, reminding one of the fire that *licked* up
the water in the trench round Elijah's sacrifice.
Rex was with the other officers, keeping an eye
on the fuel-yard which was near, and from which
soldiers were employed in sweeping away the burning embers as they fell. It was most providential
that the wind set over the river instead of over the
city, otherwise, being a dry night, high wind, and
the fire engines about as available as a boy's squirt,
probably two-thirds of the town would have gone.

An almost comical element (as one did n't suffer
one's self) was to see the spectators, who kept getting the falling sparks into their eyes, going about
with pocket-handkerchiefs to their faces. Also a
small boy who laid a complaint to Major Graham
against the soldiers who were protecting the rescued
property, because they would n't give him some
small article that belonged to him. The disgusting
part is that these fires are said to be almost always
the work of incendiaries. . . .

Your loving sister,

J. H. EWING.

17 August, 1867.
" REKA DOM," FREDERICTON.

MY DEAREST
MOTHER, — . . . Now
I must tell you all
our news. First about
the Episcopal family.
You know they have
been away for five
weeks, and we met

them first at Government House.   Since then they
have certainly done their best to make up for
lost time, in the way of kindness, and it is not
the least of the many blessings of my home here
to have such very kind people about one, as our
neighbours in general are, and such unusually
good, intellectual, and friendly friends as the Medleys.   He was a friend of John Newman, and
associated with him in working at the Lives of
the Fathers, etc., and Newman's secession was a
great grief to him.   He is awfully fond of music,
and composes chants, etc.   He is a fluent Hebrew
scholar, and is certainly, as I told you, one of the
ablest preachers I ever heard.   He has been very
near to going home to the council that is to be
held at Lambeth, only he could not make out that
the subjects of discussion had been settled, so was
not certain that it would come to much, and had
confirmations here, and did not like to bring Mrs.
Medley back in winter, for she is nearly as bad a
sailor as I am, or you might have seen them, and
heard of us.   They are *great* admirers of yours.
Especially they are devoted to the Parables.   Mrs.

Medley told me to-day they owe you so much, she
was delighted to do anything for your daughter; so
you see, dear mother, you have, so to speak, provided me a motherly friend in these distant parts.
She is a great gardener and a botanist, and litho-
graphs a little. . . . They are going away again
on a Confirmation tour directly, but meanwhile we
see them constantly ; they ask us in perpetually to
meals, and send us vegetables and flowers.   I need
hardly say that Rex and Episcopus himself are
pretty inseparable at " the instrument," and that
Rex is appointed supplementary organist, and has
joined the choir.   He is going to play at the anni-
versary festival next Sunday, and the choir generally are quite as much edified and charmed to see
the author of " Jerusalem," and quite as much as-
tonished to find (and still a little sceptical) that
" Argyle and the Isles " was not the composer, as if
we all were living in a small English watering
place.   This you would anticipate ; but you would
hardly expect to hear that the Bishop evolved and
propounded to me the proposal, that if I would
teach him German this winter, he would teach me

Hebrew.   He buys books evidently with an appetite, and will lend us *any*, so we are well off to
an extent that seems marvellous and is truly
delightful.

We have free access to the Provincial Library
here.   This is an admirable theological and grave
library, *all* Jeremy Taylor's, and almost every ordinary theological reference book, besides Greek and
Hebrew grammars and lexicons.   I am absolutely
the only member at this present time!   At the
present moment I have all " Nature and Art " (for
the water-colour lessons,) and Rex has Blunt's
" Undersigned Coincidences" from the Bishop.
I have Harding's " Lessons on Art" and a book
on colour from the Provincial, and Alex. Knox
from the Cathedral, libraries.   We only want a
modern foreign library to be perfect, so as to get
at Schiller, or *Faust* for the Bishop.   As it is, we
mean to put him through Grimm ! ! !

I am just now very busy upon an interior of the
Cathedral, at which I work, while Rex practises.
I have got some good hints from Harding's book
about drawing the arches, etc.   I got dreadfully

grieved at my stupidity over the colouring about here. I do wish I were a better artist! and Rex thinks I have gone back rather than forward. However, I have got some good books here, and I mean to work hard this winter indoors. I think my "interior" looks wonderfully promising so far.

I am going to save seed of all the wild flowers I can, and shall send it home, so have a nice sunny bit got ready to sow them in! You know what lives here will live with you, and some of the flowers are truly lovely. Spotted yellow lilies and splendid Michaelmas daisies grow wild, and a lovely white flower, something like a white foxglove (a Chelone glabra!), which I hope will seed itself like a foxglove, and so be easily grown. Beautiful spireas too; and oh! the pitcher plants grow here, but we have not seen them. One plant held four or five quarts of water, they tell us.

Your loving daughter,

J. H. EWING.

October, 1867.

MY DEAREST MOTHER, — I wish you could come
in this moment! I have got a nice wood fire in
my grate (for it is a coolish morning, one of
those clear fresh mornings that I fancy we shall
have pretty consistently through the autumn). I
am afraid I shall hardly have time this mail, but
I must make you a sketch of my room! "Sarah"
has a great admiration for my table of little
things (of which she always leaves the dusting
to me). She says "Mrs. Coster" (her former
mistress) "had a great many little things, too, not
so many as *you*, ma'am, but then she was burnt
out three times; but any little things she *did*
save she was very choice of. She saved one plate
out of her dessert service." The coolness with
which people regard being "burnt out" here is
amazing!! The day of the fire Sarah was telling
me all sorts of "burning out" anecdotes. Some
people seem to be under a sort of evil spell as
regards it. "The fire hunts him everywhere."
There is a certain man she told me of, and wherever he settles fire follows him!! One could

make a splendid Salamander story from it in the
Edgar Poe style! One comical idea one can
quite understand, viz., that as much is broken as
burnt in these fires often. Sarah told me of one
in which, in his anxiety to save, a man flung a
fine mirror out of the window into the street, *to
save it from the flames.* Of course it was smashed
to shivers!

I have got you a dial, and mean to make the
sketch, and send it herewith. It is in the garden
of a little old lady here, a Mrs. Shore. She is
very tiny and very old. She goes to the 7.30 service like clockwork, has a garden, paints life-size
portraits in oils!! and complains that, "between
housekeeping, literature, and the fine arts, she
never has time for anything." I sat with her last
night for a bit. "Do you find the days long
enough, my dear?" "Not one-half," I said; "but
they say the winter *is* long." "You will never
find it long enough, my dear."

The woods now are *lovely*. The autumn tints
are beyond describing, or colouring. One day I
began a sketch, but it is most unsatisfactory, and

now it is raining, and I am so afraid of getting
no more opportunity. A tree stands off against
a grey woody background, and it is a brilliant
yellow and crimson. Sometimes a whole tree is
canary colour, and another near it one uniform
rich deep red, another like bronze, and so on.
They are not all so by any means, of course; but
in the "College Grove," as it is called (which is
something like a beautiful bit of English pasture,
and park, and wood scenery), are the loveliest
varieties of colour.

I had a jolly drive with the Medleys the other
day. We got out and went across country a bit,
over hedges and ditches, and I sketched a little at
intervals. Once I said, "I really hope we may
be here another summer, that I may get some of
these *trees* done," and the Bishop groaned, "Don't
talk of another summer! you must stay here forever." Rex is still at the organ, and the Bishop
bristles with new chants. Rex is at work on a
Christmas anthem; words my choosing.

Recit. and Bass Solo. "And Balaam said: I
shall see him, but not now. I shall behold Him,

but not nigh. *Alto Solo.* There shall come a
Star out of Israel. (*Chorus.* A Star out of Israel).
Quartet. Thy throne, O God, is forever and ever.
A Sceptre of Righteousness is the Sceptre of
Thy Kingdom." Final chorus not decided on. I
must stop.

Your loving sister,

J. H. E.

January 26, 1868.

MY DEAREST MOTHER, — . . . I must tell you
about the sleigh drive. It was given by Col.
Harding (who is the temporary governor as well).
The etiquette of such affairs is, that the leader
drives wherever he likes, and the other sleighs must
go after him. (They say General Doyle used to
go into the most *audacious* places to try and upset
the tandems!) The young men ask the young
ladies to drive with them as they would ask them
to dance, and we old couples go Darby and Joan
together. Rex got a nice little sleigh with buffalo
robes in it, and the horse went capitally. We met
before the House of Assembly, and kept driving

round and round in circles till all assembled (about
twenty-six sleighs).   Then, bells ringing, red tassels
waving, away we went. The colonel took us in
and out about the town, but no really nasty places,
and then into the barrack-yard, where the soldiers
cheered, and his horses got so unmanageable that
he and his young lady nearly came to grief; then
out into the open country. I don't think I ever
saw anything much prettier than the line of jingling
sleighs, flying over the snowy roads, with the pure
fields of snow on all sides broken by the dark firs
and country homesteads.   Once we went up a
narrow hill meet to be drawn by Doré (or rather
Doré might give one a faint idea of its beauty),
snow pure white before us and under our feet, and
great dark firs on each side almost touching over
our heads. We stopped at a country inn, where
lunch was prepared, sandwiches and hot spiced
negus, and very jolly we were, Rex's " tscho-ga,"
which he wore over his coat, exciting considerable
admiration.

.   .   .

Do you know we mean to "flit" this May! It

will be a grief to part with the lovely views from this dear old Reka Dom, but it is too huge and too cold in winter, and burns enough fuel to — well, as one of Rex's men said, " It would take a major-general's allowance, sir ! " We have our eye on a comfortable little house close by, with garden, and eight rooms in it, and they say well-built and convenient.

Your loving daughter,

J. H. E.

22 March, 1868.

People are very kind. I was walking to church when Dr. Ward met us, going off on a professional drive. He turned out his man, took me into the sleigh, and drove me to the Cathedral before proceeding on his way, that I might not have to wade through the snow. Mrs. Shore (the lady with the dial in her garden) says (she comes regularly to the daily services with small regard to the weather) that she thinks Providence always sends somebody to help her home. In this weather she needs some one, and Rex occasionally tenders his arm !

Mrs. Shore (the dial lady) is as lively as ever. We have a little joke every day almost after morning prayers. I say, " Mrs. Shore, allow me to be your particular Providence,' and she says, " My dear, I was looking for you," and I give her my arm to take her home over the slippery ice.

EASTER TUESDAY, 1868.

Dear little Mrs. Shore I told you about. We have been so grieved the last week, as she has been very ill. On Good Friday she was given up, but with some difficulty the Bishop obtained leave to see her. They told him that it was no use, as she was unconscious etc. ; however, she revived when he went in, and he bathed her face with eau-de-cologne, and she revived; and he sent Mrs. Medley to her, who has been nursing her since, and she is now recovering. Today, *much* better.

April 26, 1868.

Poor dear little Mrs. Shore was buried on the day of the snow-storm. Such a wild day, I was not

able to go to her funeral, for which I was sorry.
The choir went in black, and sat in their places.
Rex went, and played the Dead March, and went
on to the cemetery.   I went to see her after she was
dead.   It was a lovely little face.   It is to me very
comforting to see how faces that have been marred
by the struggle of life, and disfigured by the odds
and ends of mortality (queer caps, and wrappings,
mannerisms, and traces of illness, etc.!), become
beautiful in the peace of death without becoming
unrecognizable.   Don't you know ?   I saw so clearly
what a pretty girl Mrs. Shore must have been, and
it makes one understand how hereafter one may
be beautiful, and *yet* recognized.   There were
lovely flowers in the room, and a saucer of *salt*
on her breast.   I fancy she must have been laid
out by an Irish nurse.   We all feel very much for
poor Miss Garnison; she has lost a happy home.
She will remain here a bit, and Rex will give her
some lessons on the organ.

My dearest D., — . . . Rex has got a pair of
snow shoes, and a pair are ordered for me !   Peter

Poultier, our Indian brother, guffawed loudly at
the idea of my having them, and says, "*She'll*
make *them*" (i. e., his squaw).   You should have
seen Rex wading about on the deep snow of our
garden the other night, — the Costers, Sarah, and
I watching him.   Everybody said we should tumble
down at first, and Rex said he must have out the
orderly to pick him up.   "Hartney"! "Yes, sir."
"Be ready in the garden to pick me up when I
fall!"   "Yes, sir."

Tell D. that the ankles are quite equal to snowshoeing, which is a thousand times easier than
skating, though Captain Poulton *did* yell with
laughing so loud that I told him he could be
heard at S. John.   The first time, he saw me in
them, about a quarter of a mile off, and would
give no further account of himself than "Mrs.
Ewing in snow-shoes, wading up a bank, was too
many for his feelings."   But I believe that my
"carriage" is rather graceful than otherwise on
them!   Rex says I go like a squaw, which is
really a compliment, though the gait is more

peculiar than absolutely beautiful. A sort of up-right, easy swing of a walk!!!

.　　　.　　　　.　　　.

I hope Rex's Easter Anthem will be very successful. It begins with a *Bass Recit. Solo:* "Very early in the morning on the first day of the week, they came unto the sepulchre." (*Trio* of women's voices): "They have taken away the Lord, and we know not where they have laid Him." (*Alto Solo* — Angel): "Why seek ye the living among the dead? He is not here." (*Chorus*): "He is not here. He is risen." (*Chorus*): "He is risen." It ends with a full chorale: "Christ is risen from the dead, and is become the first-fruits of them that slept. Alleluia, Amen."

Rex has got some lovely songs lately. A lot of Franz's and of Schumann's. The way those men "marry music" to Heine's "immortal verse" is wonderful. You really would enjoy the exquisite delicacy with which some of Heine's gems are set.

FIRST SUNDAY AFTER EPIPHANY, 1868.

The other night I looked out and saw that the
moon was shining on the snow, looking exactly
as if the river had opened, and there was a water-
surface. This was because the intense frost had
crusted and glazed the snow on the river so that
it reflected. Meanwhile a high wind was blowing
what *loose* snow there was in white wreaths hither
and thither. The Indians, by the bye, call Feb-
ruary "the moon in which there is crust on the
snow." One really hardly knows what snow is in
England. It is so dry here it is like dust, and is
blown about the streets. It takes a considerable
time to melt when you get it into the house, and
of course does not wet your feet or clothes out
of doors unless it is thawing. We keep little
brooms in the halls here to brush the snow from
our feet and clothes when we come into a house.
November is called "the moon in which the frost
fish comes," by which I suppose are meant the
"cusks" (as they call them here), a very nice fish
we get when the river closes. The men cut
holes in the ice and get them out. I don't know

the process, though I have seen them in the distance. I suppose the fish come to the hole attracted by the light, but I don't know. Rex says they had them in the north of China.

.   .   .   .   .

18 March, 1868.

The bull dog is just barking at the avalanches of snow that keep shooting off the roof with a roar like thunder. For we are in the middle of a thaw, and after being about 35° below zero last Monday morning, to-day it is 50° above, and the ice is beginning to thaw upon the river; however, I fancy it will all harden up again. A priest was ordained to-day, and there were two awful avalanches during service. *Such* a noise it does make. The musical abilities of our clergy were brought into effective use to-day, for they and the Bishop sang their own lines of the Veni Creator, the choir singing the alternate ones. The effect was really most impressive. Coster's fine bass, Mr. Pearson's sweet tenor, etc., and the Bishop's hearty voice support alternate lines with ample power, and it was very pretty, the men's voices, as they all stood round the new priest, and then the response of the choir. It was to a simple old psalm tune.

I must add to my list of friends our new neighbours, or rather " Over-the-ways " — two very old ladies who were among the first settlers. (The Loyalists came here and " settled " in Fredericton in 17 — alas! I forget; 88 I think). There was one old wooden church in those days, and terrible battles about pews, which were put up to auction in the church, and principal residents insisting on having pews of double size. The parson lived on the other side of the river, and one day he came over in a birch-bark canoe and went back the same way, and was never heard of again. Miss Bailey remembers that on June 1st, being the King's birthday, they fired cannon over the river to raise the body, but it was not found for eight days. When the Bishop came, people went, once to church on Sunday, and in the afternoon paid visits and played cards. You may imagine the storm created by his insisting on free seats.

July 7, 1868.

. . . How I wish for you on moonlight nights in
the canoe.   The other night we went out before
sunset and stayed late.   The sunset was wonderful,

ON THE
NASHWAAK
RIVER.

and whilst the crimson was still deluging the sky
and river, the moon looked through it like a ghost.
We went up the Nashwaak Cis (Little Nashwaak,
a tributary of S. John), and *lay to* close to a large
green bullfrog, who looked at us, but never moved.
A bittern was groaning in the ferns by the bank
(masses of Onoclea), and song birds were singing
everywhere.   We came out into the S. John as the

moon rose, and finally two other canoes joined us, and we flew up and down through the water, and then lay to and listened to the 22nd band through the mess room windows.   Does n't it seem funny to you to fancy *me* paddling on a great beautiful river like this ?   Rex and I go alone now (I bow, he stern), and enjoy ourselves amazingly —

August 29, 1868.

. . . How thankful I am that my letters *have* somewhat counteracted the Bishop's vivid description of the climate ! In this glorious autumn weather it does indeed seem a " need not " for you to be distressing yourself, as you sit in the fogs of dear old Yorkshire, about us in our bright clear atmosphere. . . . For a short sojourn, and with no necessity for fifty miles' journeys in sleighs and such-like fatiguing expeditions, we are simply unspeakably fortunate in the climate. I hope I told you that snowshoeing is an *amusement*, like *skating*, and that there is no more necessity for me to snowshoe on this river than there ever was for me to skate on the dam ! I thoroughly enjoy it. People

make parties to snowshoe, and splendid fun it is.
Why, WE PICNIC in the winters here, which is more
than you do at home! Picnic in the woods, and
hot spiced claret supersedes champagne cup!
And sometimes girls meet and make *snowhouses*,
inside which you are as warm as an Esquimaux.
I talked of having one last winter to sketch from,
and this one perhaps I shall! . . .

Monday, 31. Such a lovely day! As Mrs.
Medley said to me this morning as we came out
of church, "It is a *splendid* climate! We have so
few dull days, so many clear bright ones!" Did
I tell you of our latest picnic? No. It was the
jolliest we have had, I think. We took the Parrys
in our canoe. I had a little funked it, it was so
hot, and I sometimes get a headache from the sun,
and when we paddle against stream and wind I
can't use an umbrella, and we had a good many
miles to go about midday. But we found an old
"puggaree" of Rex's, of Constantinople days,
fastened it on to my hat, and it answered *perfectly*.

We had a charming day. I did a little sketch-
ing, and we came home by moonlight, fourteen

canoes lashed together. We were in the middle,
so Rex and Capt. P. were idle, except that Rex
" conducted " the singing with a paddle! We had
a good many comic songs, and some part singing.
The most interesting to me was a song sung by
Gabriel, the Indian, a curious wild, monotonous,
plaintive affair, but wonderfully in keeping with
the motion of the canoes, and the plash of the
water in the moonlight.

October 12, 1868.

MY DEAREST D. : — The paper is up !!! I leave
you to imagine my feelings. I told you how Mrs.
Medley and I had felt ourselves cut out by
" Bluenoses " when we found that Mrs. D. and
Miss P. could *paper* and we could not! Where-
upon (having found a cheap paper in a stationer's
shop where Rex was music-hunting) I determined
to paper our dining-room; and as Mrs. D. was
on a visit to Mrs. M., I called to draw out a few
incidental instructions in the course of conversation!! I found Mrs. M. had been before me, and
had papered a closet !!! The two ladies an-

nounced their intention of calling in to see how
I got on, and after church on Friday morning,
having borrowed steps of Mrs. L. and an old
whitewash brush of Mrs. C., and having *cut* a
good many rolls of paper over night, I donned
my old blue print, and sent for the orderly to take
out the picture nails. He began — " When the
man that 's going to paper comes, ma'am " — and
I felt very proud to shut him up with " *I 'm* the
man that 's going to paper, Hartney " (in a parlia-
mentary sense of man ! !). Just then the bell rang,
and he came back with a very solemn face — " It 's
the Bishop's lady, mum !! " — leaving her at the
door. However, the B.'s lady and Mrs. D. ended
by working with me till lunch, which, though it
diminishes my credit, decidedly accelerated the
work. They were intensely good, and we got
fully half done. Next day Mrs. D. and Miss J.
came and helped me, and late on Saturday evening
I finished it off myself. I think it looks quite as
well as the other papers.

S. John's Day, 1868.

. . . I will tell you how we spent our Christmas. It did not *promise* very brightly, for the cold which seemed to hang so unaccountably about me, turned out to be a sort of epidemic variety of influenza, i. e. influenza, without any cold in the head, but feverish discomfort and a sort of throat affection, something like mumps in a mild form outside, and swelling within also; in fact, " mumps, lumps, and dumps " about sums it up! " Everybody" has had it. . . . I did not get to church on Christmas Day, but that was our only drawback, and we were so jolly and comfortable that we had a delightful day. On Christmas Eve we were sitting on the landing by the dumbstove, when (very late) a ring came at the door, and a parcel was put into Rex's hands by an unknown " party." It was a very pretty plated coffee pot, and ditto butter cooler, with a note to the effect that some members of the choir begged him to accept this little Christmas gift as a very small mark of their gratitude for his kindness in taking so much trouble with them. This was rather a pleas-

ant beginning to Christmas, was n't it? Rex had
previously dressed the house with some "pricknig"
thoughtfully sent by Mrs. Medley, and had carried
me round the house to see the effect. I had had
some fun sending Hetty shopping for our turkey
and various odds and ends of Christmasings. On
Christmas eve, also, " Peter Poultice," our Indian
brother, gave us a call, and Rex took the opportunity to buy me a pair of bead-worked moccasins,
the first smart pair I have had. Then I sent
him up the town to his favourite "store" to buy
a piece of music as a Christmas box from me to him,
and he returned with "Israel in Egypt," and an
American stereoscope for *me.* . . . Then in the
evening Rex went downstairs and played "Chris-
tians, awake" lovelily with all kinds of stops and
different effects, and I sat upstairs by the dumbstove, and was not entirely in Canada, as you may
fancy! He did this for me last year. When he
had done he came up again, and said he hoped he
would play that for me every Christmas Eve, wherever we were, even when he was an old man and
his old fingers trembled on the keys. It was after

that the testimonial came. Then the R. C. bell began to chime for midnight Mass, and Hetty went to bed, and Rex read the evening service with me as Christmas Eve passed into Christmas Day. . . .

I am at this moment waiting for the Bishop, with whom I am going to communicate with the "Loyalist Ladies." They are two *very* old ladies who live in a cottage opposite. Their father was one of the loyalist Americans who left the States to settle in Canada when the States rebelled; I mean in the *old* American War. They were some of the first settlers in Fredericton. The two sisters are a single lady (Miss Bailey) and a widow (Mrs. Emmerson). They called me their "little neighbour," and are pleased to look very favourably on me, and they like me to come when they receive the Holy Communion, which they do from time to time, as they never go out now. I accuse Rex of a penchant for Miss B. and a flirtation from his dressing-room window. She is immensely old, ninety — something, but *on dit* that she does not like it to be supposed that she is so old. However, she likes me, though I *was* injudicious enough to

enquire how the first French Revolution affected
this Province from her experience! . . .

April 10, 1869.

. . . Rex has been appointed conductor of the
Choral Society. There have been two nights
under the new bâton, and the people are delighted.
" We " are to give a concert shortly, and you shall
have a programme. Rex is writing a thing with
an " invisible chorus " on the words of Miss Proc-
ter's " Vision." Mr. Roberts (basso profundo) is
to take the first part (solo), half the chorus is to
take the mourner's song " on the stage," Mrs.
Rowan (soprano) is to take the second part (solo),
and the other half of the chorus will sing the
Angels' song " behind the scenes." I am to be
with the party in front so as to hear the invisible
chorus. It seems so strange to have so much to
do with concerts and choir here, and not to be
able to have any of *you* in them! I want the ladies
to be dressed in uniform, and hope it may come to
pass. We shall probably all be in white, with
different coloured ribbons for sopranos and altos.

9

April 17, 1869.

MY DEAREST FATHER, — I wanted to adorn your
letter, but I fear I have not succeeded. The illustra-
tion is by way of giving you an idea of the finest
"aurora" I have ever seen. I have been a little
disappointed with the want of colour in the auroras
I have seen here hitherto, and they have only
occupied part of the heavens; but on the 15th,
from 8 to 9 P. M. (with *us*) the above was visible,
and poured from the zenith to the horizon, north,
south, east, and west. In the west the rays were
beautifully coloured, and the sky looked as rosy
as after sunset *or* a fire in the woods. Against
this the " young moon in the old moon's lap " over
the dark chimney tops of the Rectory, was certainly
a lovely sight. The magnetic storm seemed to
rage in some places, and the general brilliancy
faded from time to time, and then burst out again
in vivid streams at particular points. It began in
the south, and passed northwards, not a usual
thing *here*. In fact, it was altogether more like an
Australian aurora, Rex says. *The* lovely (or

rather *grand*) feature was the corona at the zenith above our heads. It changed as ceaselessly as the rays, — sometimes obscured. A dark mass would suddenly *rift* with an effect like one of Martin's boldest imaginations in his Milton. The rays were sharpest near the corona, and then again near the horizon. It was like standing under a tent of celestial proportions, where the curtains showed light and shadow as they rustled. Occasionally in the west the rosy tint was mixed with greenish and yellow rays, never very brilliant that we saw, but we did not see it at the very best, I believe. . . The Bishop said he had not seen such a one for twenty years.

ROSE HALL, FREDERICTON, N. B.
8 May, 1869.

. . . This is our new nest; it is a lovely summer resting place. We take it by the month, and there seems a fair prospect of our not having to move at any rate for two or three months, but there is no certain news for anybody as yet. . . . We get more and more pleased with our present arrangements.

It is a great point to have big airy rooms in the hot summer here.[1]

June 14, 1869.

We have at last had a John Gilpin jaunt in our honeymoon, and it *has* been enjoyable. . . The contractor for the board of the men on lookout for deserters to the States, stationed at the outpost at Eel River, having fortunately chosen this lovely season for failing to fulfil his contract, Rex had to go there on business, and I accompanied him for pleasure! . . . We had never been "up river" before, except ten miles or so in canoe. The "boats" only run in the spring and autumn freshets. We left here at 5.15 A. M., and got to Eel River about 2 P. M. (sixty miles or so). It was lovely, though the "black fly" hardly left us alive! We spent the night at the inn, took the boat again on Tuesday morning, and came *down river* (forty-eight or fifty miles down). *I* landed at Crock's Point, where Mr. Dowling met me in his "wagon"

[1] These desolate ruins are all that are now left of the Rose Hall Mrs. Ewing knew and loved, as the place was destroyed by fire some seven years ago.

RUINS OF "ROSE HALL" TO-DAY.

(the four-wheeled " gig " of the country), and Rex
went on to Fredericton for the Choral Society's
practice. At Douglas we had some dinner, and in
the afternoon Mr. D. having to visit a sick man in
his Keswick district, he, I, and Mrs. Dowling
squeezed into the wagon and drove eighteen miles
through *lovely* country, on *such* a beautiful evening.
I saw the Keswick Church (to the consecration of
which Rex went in the winter of 1867), a *very* nice
little one. Coming back poor Mr. D. had " hard
times " of it with me and his wife, for we had
brought a trowel, and we found "ladies' slippers "
and other treasures not so common close at hand,
and it seemed very doubtful if we could get home
before dark, though it is midsummer! Old " King,"
Mrs. D.'s dog, was with us and enjoyed himself greatly. When we came in, we found Mr.
Hannington en route home from a drive in *his*
wagon. People exercise unlimited hospitality of
its quiet kind in the country, and he stayed all
night. We *meant* to go to bed very early, but we
ended in sitting up rather early! in the study,
discussing Tennyson, Handel, miracle plays,

Jeremy Taylor, table turning, etc. Somebody
promised to " call " Mr. H., who had to drive fifteen
or sixteen miles to Jones's Island, where Rex was
to be deposited by the morning boat from Fredericton. Happily he called himself, for we were
all too thoroughly done up to wake early. Mrs. D.
and I went out and botanized till a little after
dinner time, and then she and I got into the
wagon, packed my traps, took King, and bid
Douglas adieu, and drove to Prince William. It
is about sixteen miles, and, as we had a " wait " at
the ferry, we did not get there till 8 P. M., when the
Hanningtons and Rex had almost given us up.
They had a roast turkey for us, and we had a capital dinner and were much refreshed, but so sleepy
all the evening that I discovered as in a dream that
Mr. Hannington was prizeman for botany at the
college here, and that he exhibited to me a very
ingenious press, and gave me some splendid specimens of brown trillium. Again we all faithfully
promised to " call " each other, and rolled into bed.
We started off again next day, Mr. H. and I
packed into his wagon, Mrs. Dowling and Mrs. H.

into the Dowlings'; Rex rode the spare horse, and
away we went. It was a twenty miles' drive, and
part of the time the sun was very hot, and I had
to take off my grey cloak and put the table cloth
round me to turn the sun. As we crept up the last
hill (through country more like our moors, saving
that the hills and slopes are covered not with
heather but the illimitable forest), Mr. H. wildly
begged me to shut my eyes. I kept them closed
till we were on the summit and by the church. It
looks down on —— " Killarney on a larger scale,"
says Rex, the distant ranges not so high in propor-
tion, but a wide, wide beautiful lake, dotted with fir
covered islands deep down in the valley below the
church. On the other side it looks down on an
ocean of unbroken forest, softening into purple and
blue with distance, but "woods, woods, woods."
Against this background far down the little quaint,
white-painted Magundy Church shines like a star;
around the church is a churchyard (if you knew
how often settlers bury their people in their own
gardens, etc., as if they were their old horses or pet
dogs, you would know the value of the sight!) full

of white stones and with clumps of the apple-green
osmundas on the graves. All Saints will be a
very pretty church. (N. B. — It is not built of *logs*,
but of wood like the houses, and very pretty.) It
is roofed in, and is to be consecrated in September.
One grave is already in the churchyard, among the
wild strawberry blossom and the fern, that of a very
good girl and a communicant. We picnicked in the
valley below the lovely trees. Then we went on
to the lake, and it is lovely. The shore is gleaming
white sand (*porphyry*, says Mr. H., and it is lovely
stuff; I brought a handkerchief full to put in my
aquarium). Out of the sand grow blueberry plants.
Mr. H. "whipped off" his shoes and stockings
and walked about so along the shore. When we
returned our horse had escaped, and the men had
to hunt for him. I dug up flower roots with
dogged persistency, though the mosquitos and
black fly bit me till I rushed madly to the lunch
basket, grabbed the butter, smeared my face and
hands all over, and — went back to the trilliums!
Tell Stephen I saw fourteen different species of
fern that I knew in that one drive, and I got

pitcher plants (full of rain water!), etc. Well, we
got our horses, Mr. H. rode, and Rex drove me.
When we got back to All Saints I went over it,
and then went back into it again to use it as a
house of prayer for once, for the strange, sad feeling
is we shall probably never see it again. Coming
out, I found that Rex had been adjuring the old
iron grey " Dolly " on the subject of men and
beasts praising the Lord.   He is delighted with the
church, and he and I are to give the prayer desk.
One of the people had prepared a tea for us at
Magundy, so we did not get home till nearly midnight, and twenty miles in the dark, through woods,
do seem *uncommonly* long.   Next day we drove
to the river bank, canoed to Jones's Island, took
the boat, and came home.

July 11, 1869.

. . . On Wednesday evening I had the Cathedral Choir and the members of Rex's Friday class
to tea, nearly forty people.   I went into the
market and secured a lot of the wild strawberries,
which are just beginning, butter, etc., borrowed
china and glass of my friends, and all went off

very successfully. The music (it was a practice)
was very good. I wish you could hear the movement from Rex's anthem of " When the Lord
turned again the captivity of Sion " — " He that
now goeth on his way weeping." Mrs. Rowan
sings it beautifully, and the chorus of " They
that sow in tears shall reap in joy" was really
fine. . . .   '

July has been altogether an exciting month to
us. The paper I send will speak for itself as to
the second concert, which was *most* successful.
I only wanted some of your dear old faces to
reflect *my* pride and pleasure at the way people
heaped praise and applause on Rex's head. Mr.
Roberts broke down in reading the address, which
I now keep in a sacred drawer. It is a most ele-
gant affair, tied with red ribbon. But *the* upsetting thing was when the Bishop left the audience
and came up on to the platform. He had known
nothing about it, and his " say " was of course all
impromptu ; the newspaper does it no manner of
justice. When he turned his loving face on Rex
to bid him good bye, it was — well, what the

whole thing was — almost more than one could
bear. We are going to scramble in another concert before the month is out, if all be well, and
we suspect there is to be another " demonstra-
tion " then ! !

10 August, 1869.

FREDERICTON, N. B^x.

OUR VERY DEAR MOTHER, — We would fain
spare *you* the uncertainty which is the shady side
of our wandering life. But (as we have often
reason to say) " one can't have everything." Up
to yesterday afternoon we hoped and believed that
this very day we should begin the journey that,
please God, is to end in the old nest; but it is
not to be for a little bit yet. We hope, however,
that it *is* only deferred for a few weeks. We felt
rather " knocked over " yesterday evening, but all
right to-day. I *had* rather dwelt on the joy of
sending you a telegram from Liverpool in place of
a letter across the Atlantic; but still we feel keenly
enough how much — how very much — we have
to be grateful for; and *if we are* allowed to go

home this time, I shall make few grumbles as to route, vessel, everything else, I promise you!

. . . On Tuesday evening the Choral Society gave a small concert, where Sir James Carter sat smiling in the front ranks, and Major Cox sat meditative by the door! After the Hallelujah Chorus, the Bishop came forward and in the name of the society gave Rex a silver cup and a watch chain. The cup is very light and artistic, very pretty indeed, and beautifully engraved with an inscription on one side, and a " design " of musical instruments on the other. The chain is simple and pretty. The people were wonderfully kind, and are forever bemoaning our departure. . . . It is *very* pleasant to get a kind word and a hearty regret from every tradesman one pays off and every friend we say good bye to. . . . Poor Mrs. Medley broke down so bitterly in congratulating me on going home to *my mother*, — " She will be so proud of you both, and the love you have won here!" and the poor soul sobbed, and did I *not* sympathize?

. . . Did I ever tell you of the Bishop's present

to Rex? — two huge splendid volumes of Anthems, etc., by Purcell and others, published by the Motet Society, with an inscription in the first page, —

" To Alexander Ewing, from his sincere friend, John Fredericton. In remembrance of many happy hours spent in the Service of the Church of God."

I am very proud of it, and it is a valuable work in many ways.

Letter to Major Ewing after the passing away
of his beloved wife, in 1885.

FREDERICTON,
ST. JOHN BAPTIST'S DAY, 1885.

MY DEAR MAJOR EWING, — I hope I need not
assure you of our true sympathy under the heavy
affliction you have sustained, and our heartfelt
sorrow for a loss felt by thousands besides ourselves. We have long feared that your dear wife
would break down under the mental strain of
writing what gave such infinite pleasure, not only
to children, but to grown persons, and yet we felt
sure that it was a fire that could not be restrained,
and that the mind of true genius would consume the
frail body. We have followed as well as we could
every step as mourners, and through the " Guar-
dian " we seemed to be part of the procession and
to bear a bunch of flowers, though the wide sea
rolls between us. I never pass the little white
cottage without thinking of you both as we all
sat down to read a chapter in Hebrew, and we

shall never have again one to lead us in the choir as you used to do.

We have had two other losses of dear friends this year, — one most distressing, Col. F. Strangways, and by the last mail we hear of the death of Archdeacon Woolcombe, an old Exeter friend. Our circle is indeed narrowing to a very small space. Will you accept our kind love and sympathy, and please to convey the same to her sister, who, I understand, is still with you, and believe me

Your sincere friend,   JOHN FREDERICTON.

MRS. EWING'S TOMB AT TRULL.

" . . . It is the good, and not the great things, of my life that bring me peace: or, rather, neither one nor the other, but the undeserved mercies of my God!" — FRIEDERICH'S BALLAD.

www.ingramcontent.com/pod-product-compliance
Lightning Source LLC
Chambersburg PA
CBHW020011030726
47500CB00002B/538